Pirate Nell's Tale to Tell

A Storybook Adventure

Helen Docherty & Thomas Docherty

Author and Illustrator of *The Snatchabook*

sourcebooks
jabberwocky

For Ruth, Rose and Kathie,
and for librarians everywhere!

Text © 2020 by Helen Docherty
Illustrations © 2020 by Thomas Docherty
Cover and internal design © 2020 by Sourcebooks

The full color art was created with acrylic ink and hot-pressed watercolor paper.

Published by Sourcebooks Jabberwocky, an imprint of Sourcebooks Kids
P.O. Box 4410, Naperville, Illinois 60567–4410
(630) 961-3900
sourcebookskids.com

Library of Congress Cataloging-in-Publication Data is on file with the publisher.

Source of Production: PrintPlus Limited, Shenzhen, Guangdong Province, China
Date of Production: May 2020
Run Number: 5018444

Printed and bound in China.
PP 10 9 8 7 6 5 4 3 2 1

The day Nell joined the pirate crew
was full of hope; a dream come true!

For great adventures filled her head
from every tale she'd ever read.

Nell wondered what she ought to pack.
Of course! Her Pirate's Almanac.
It taught her all she'd need to know
from how to steer to how to row;
which way was east and which was west…

but Captain Gnash was not impressed.
"An almanac?" He curled his lip.
"No time for reading on this ship!"

The other pirates warmed to Nell.
They loved the stories she would tell…

of buried chests and treasure maps,

ferocious storms and thunderclaps,

of daring rescues out at sea…

…but sadly, in reality,
Nell's days were filled with boring chores
like scrubbing pots and mopping floors,

while Captain Gnash snapped, with a sneer,
"You've missed some bird poop, over here!"

One night, Nell found it hard to sleep.
She gazed into the ocean deep,
then closed her eyes and made a wish…
At once, she saw a school of fish
all dancing, leaping, filled with light,
guiding something through the night.

Nell gasped. "Is that for me?" she cried.

"A bottle…with a map inside!"
An island, shaped like this, but where?

A secret treasure, buried there…
Adventure lay ahead, it seemed!
And through the starry night, Nell dreamed.

But when she woke, at break of day,
Nell's dreams were cruelly snatched away.
Her map was gone and, in its place,
she saw the Captain's puzzled face.

"What's this?" he ordered, with a frown.
"I think," said Nell, "it's upside down."

"Don't tell me how to read a map,
you good-for-nothing whippersnap!
There's treasure here, that's plain to see,
and don't forget: it's all for ME!"

They sailed due east; the sky was red.
Nell warned, "There might be storms ahead…"

But Captain Gnash's greedy eyes
were firmly focused on his prize.
The clouds grew dark. The waves rose high.
A sheet of lightning lit the sky.

Then Captain Gnash (who clutched the map) was startled by a thunderclap.

He lost his balance, slipped, and fell headfirst into the stormy swell!

Nell grabbed a float. Then, with a splash, she dived in after Captain Gnash.

The waves were wild, the current strong.
Nell knew she didn't have that long…

With luck, she'd studied what to do
(in "Saving Lives" page forty-two).

No sooner had she hauled him out,
Nell heard the other pirates shout.
"Oh no!" The ship had headed towards
a line of rocks like jagged swords!

Nell seized the wheel, and deftly steered…
and all the other pirates cheered!

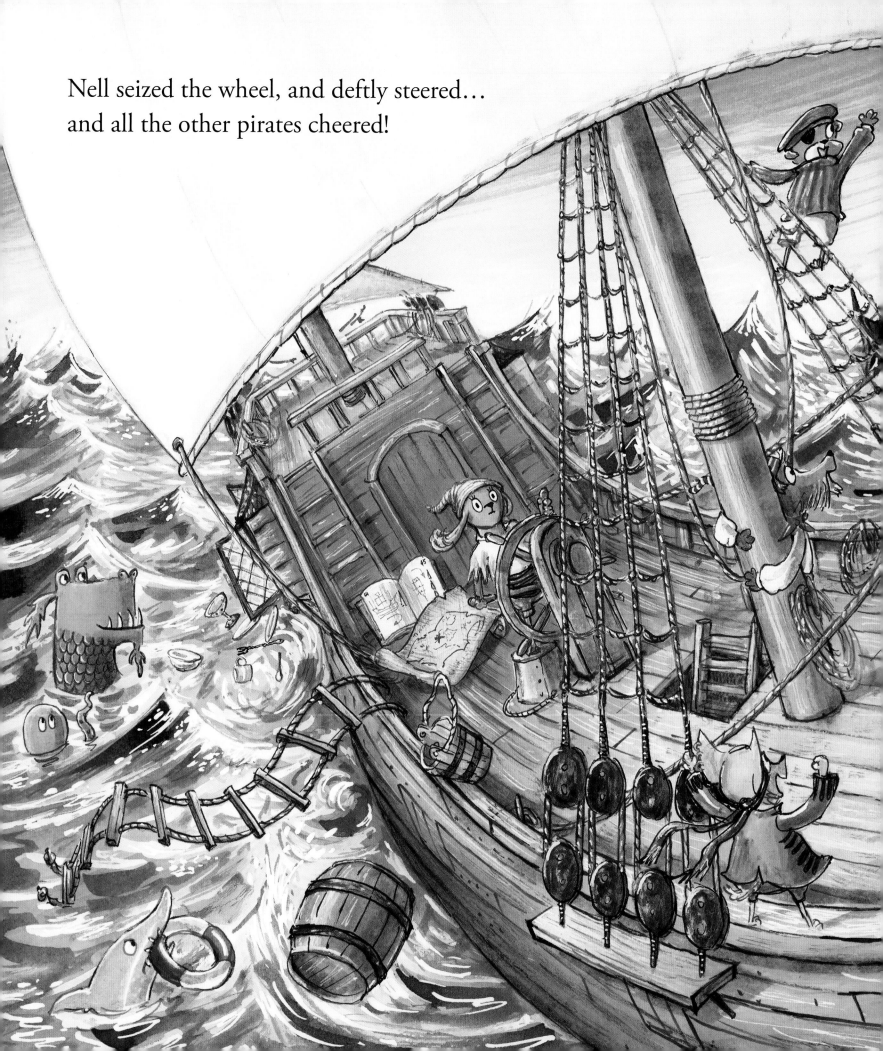

She led them safely through the storm.
The sea grew calm; the air grew warm.
The treasure map was barely dry
when something distant caught Nell's eye.
Some craggy cliffs, a sandy shore…

The island they'd
been searching for!

With map in hand, Nell led the way
to where the buried treasure lay.

The pirates dug beneath the ground.
Not one, but twenty chests they found!

What treasure lay inside, unclaimed?
"Well, bless my bootstraps!" Nell exclaimed.

The crew exchanged bewildered looks.
"So…where's the treasure?
These are…BOOKS!"

Nell told them what she'd known for ages:
"There's treasure right here in these pages!
These books are like a magic key
to other worlds, beyond the sea.
They'll whiz you off to places new.
They'll make you gasp, and giggle too.
They'll teach you things you never knew!"

"She's right, you know," the Captain said.
"Without Nell's book, we might be dead!"

"I'll teach you all to read," said Nell.
"Then you can read these books as well!"

And, being Nell, she kept her word.

She's even opened (so I've heard)
a library floating on the sea
that lends out books to all, for free!

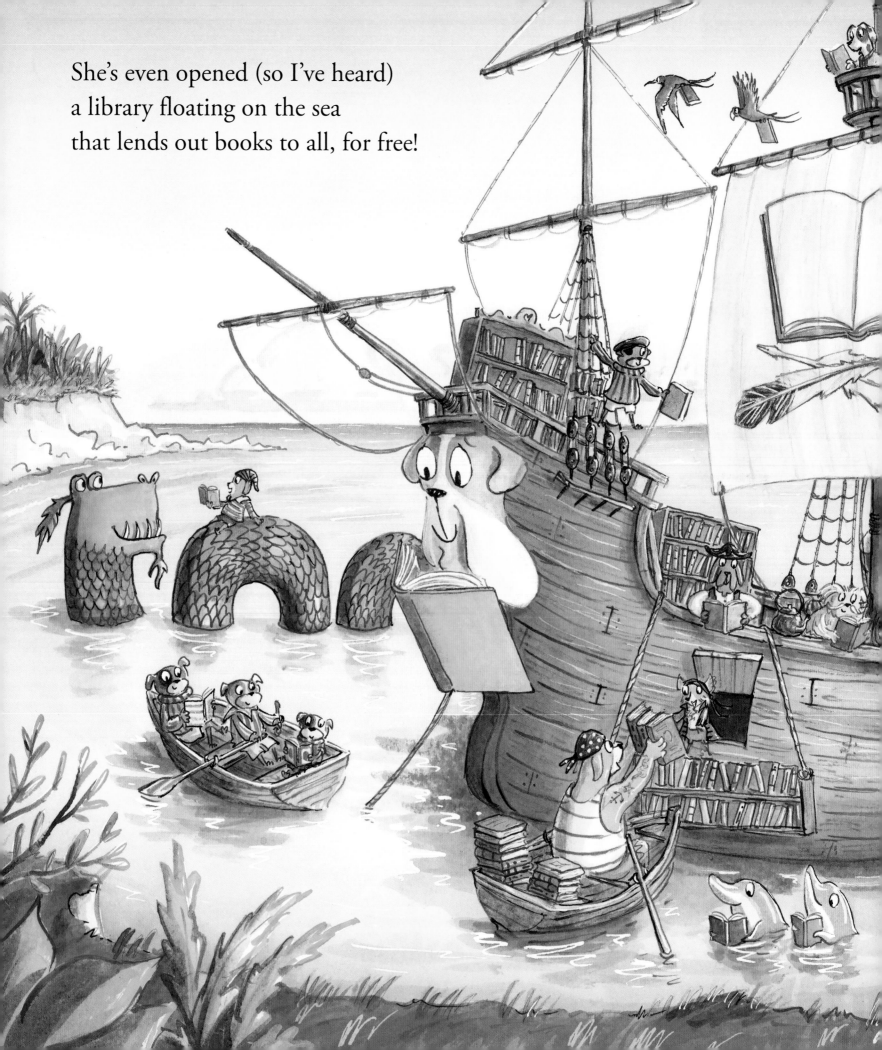

And Captain Gnash? He's changed his ways,
for now he likes to spend his days
devouring stories, back to back…
or studying Nell's Almanac.